DO NOT REMOVE
CARDS FROM POCKET

9-96

THE DINOSAURS

PREHISTORIC
NORTH AMERICA

THE DINOSAURS

RICHARD KRUEGER
ILLUSTRATED BY TED FINGER

THE MILLBROOK PRESS ■ BROOKFIELD, CONNECTICUT

Library of Congress Cataloging-in-Publication Data
Krueger, Richard.
The dinosaurs / by Richard Krueger ; illustrations by Ted Finger.
p.   cm. — (Prehistoric North America)
Includes bibliographical references and index.
Summary: The Age of Dinosaurs — how paleontologists reconstruct
this prehistoric world, the characteristics and behavior of many
different kinds of dinosaurs, and theories about their extinction.
ISBN 1-56294-548-3 (lib. bdg.)
1. Dinosaurs — Juvenile literature.   [1. Dinosaurs.]   I. Finger,
Ted, ill.   II. Title.   III. Series.
QE862.D5K67   1995   567.9′1 — dc20   94-46552   CIP   AC

Published by The Millbrook Press, Inc.
2 Old New Milford Road, Brookfield, Connecticut 06804

250 MILLION YEARS AGO

the Triassic Period began. The animals of this period were primitive two-legged meat eaters.

208 MILLION YEARS AGO

the Jurassic Period (the Age of Dinosaurs) began. Sauropods—gigantic animals with long necks and small heads—were plant eaters who walked on four legs.

145 MILLION YEARS AGO

the Cretaceous Period began. Plant-eating armored and horned dinosaurs fought for survival with meat-eating giants.

65 MILLION YEARS AGO

the dinosaurs were gone. The Age of Mammals began. Early placentals evolved into the ancestors of the modern horse.

37 MILLION YEARS AGO

the creodonts (early meat-eating mammals) began to give way to the carnivores, such as the tree-climbing dawn dog, whose descendents include wolves, coyotes, and modern dogs.

2 MILLION YEARS AGO

during the Ice Age, huge, hearty animals such as wooly mammoths lived in large numbers near the glaciers of what is now Canada and the northern United States.

12,000 YEARS AGO

human beings followed herds of animals across the Bering Land Bridge into North America.

The animal pushed its small, narrow head through the thorny branches, scraping some of the dust off its huge arched back. Its four elephantlike feet crushed the dry plants as it moved slowly forward. At last it found some tender green leaves at the center of a large fern. It clipped them with its long toothless beak. Tiny teeth in the rear of its jaw chopped the soft plants into pieces small enough to swallow.

As the hungry plant eater stretched forward to reach the last green leaves, it was startled by the sound of breaking branches. Its great body heaved upward, lifting its head 14 feet (4 meters) above the ground. The creature balanced on its long hind legs and short, thick tail as its eyes searched the forest. It watched branches moving in some nearby trees. Then it saw a huge head in the shadows. The terrified plant eater turned its bulky body and ran toward the open plain beyond the forest. The large upright plates along its back ripped leaves and branches from trees. It lumbered out of the forest and stopped. Its mouth was open, and its ribs heaved with every breath. It held its powerful tail with its two pairs of sharp spikes high in the air.

The predator was right behind, running quickly on two long legs. It charged with its mouth open and claws outstretched. The plant eater swung its spiked tail with great force against its attacker. The ferocious

ALLOSAURUS
STEGOSAURUS

meat eater roared with pain as it staggered sideways. One of the sharp tail spikes had made a deep wound in its leg.

The giant hunter began to move around its prey. It tried to get closer to the plant eater's small head and neck. Its powerful jaws were filled with sharp, slicing teeth. But the plant eater always turned with its tail held high, ready to strike. After several more tries, the wounded meat eater gave up. It limped painfully off into the forest.

The plant eater walked out onto the dusty plain. It stopped, stretched its short, thick neck, and lowered its head. A long, low rattling sound came from its throat. A moment later, its call was answered from a distant grove of trees. The animal turned and walked slowly to join others of its kind.

These two animals lived in western North America 150 million years ago. They were reptiles, but they were not like any reptiles that live in North America today. Scientists have named the 25-foot-long (7.5-meter) plant eater *Stegosaurus*. It was hunted by the fierce 35-foot-long (11-meter) *Allosaurus*. These two reptiles belong to a family of prehistoric animals called dinosaurs. They died out, or became extinct, about 65 million years ago.

How then do we know anything about them? How do we even know for certain they existed? Because they left us a record, not a written one, but a physical one. The bones and teeth of these amazing reptiles were preserved in rocks as fossils. The eggs that dinosaurs laid were also preserved as fossils.

Scientists called paleontologists have dug up the fossilized bones of dinosaurs. By studying these fossils, they learn when and where dinosaurs lived, what they ate, and how they looked. Paleontology is a way to re-create the age of dinosaurs, when fantastic, gigantic animals ruled the Earth.

FOSSILS TELL STORIES

All dinosaurs lived on land. They lived in forests, on plains, and in river valleys. Like animals living now, they died from sickness, accidents, or attacks by hungry meat eaters. Only a few of the millions of dinosaurs that once roamed North America became fossils. They were the ones that died in places where their remains were quickly covered by sediments such as mud and sand. This usually happened along riverbanks or in lakes. The skeletons that became fossilized were buried under many layers of sediment and lay undisturbed for millions of years.

Deep underground, the bones were slowly changed. Water moving through the sediments carried minerals into the bones, filling tiny open spaces called pores. This made the fossilized bones hard and heavy. The layers of sediment that contained the bones were cemented together by minerals. Sand became sandstone, and mud turned into shale. Rocks that have been made this way are called sedimentary rocks.

Most fossils are hidden underground within rocks. But here and there fossil-rich sedimentary rocks lie at the surface. Paleontologists and fossil collectors locate fossil-bearing rocks by looking at geological maps. The maps are colored to show all of the different kinds of rocks at the surface or just beneath the soil.

Most fossils are found by walking and looking. In the dry "badlands" that stretch from South Dakota to Montana, and up through Alberta, Canada, the search is easier because there is very little soil and plant cover. Each year, rainstorms wear, or erode, away rock in the badlands, and new fossils are exposed. In areas where there is deep soil and a lot of plant growth, fossil hunters find exposed sedimentary rocks along riverbanks or in man-made road cuts.

Usually bits of broken fossilized bone are found first. If larger pieces of bone are found, they are examined to see if they are worth collecting. Loose material around the bones is carefully removed. The specimen is photographed and the "dig" is mapped.

Larger specimens are removed in blocks of rock. First, the bones are covered with wet tissue paper, then the whole block is wrapped in cloth strips soaked in wet plaster. When this plaster jacket is hard, the block is pried loose from the surrounding rock and transported to a laboratory for preparation.

In the laboratory, the protective jacket is taken off. Specially trained technicians look through a microscope as they chip carefully at the remaining rock around the bones with dental tools. It might take as long as a week to clean one small bone.

Experts often study specimens for years. Skulls and teeth are especially important in this work. Leg, arm, hip, and shoulder bones often have small raised ridges where muscles were attached to them. These give useful information about the shape, size, and position of a dinosaur's muscles. The joints between the bones are studied to learn about the body's movement.

If a specimen is unusual, it may be displayed in a museum as a cast—usually made of strong, light plastic. The cast bones are drilled and mounted on steel rods in a lifelike position. The real bones are placed on storage shelves so paleontologists can continue to study them.

Scientists have a special system for naming rocks and fossils according to their age. Rocks from the age of dinosaurs are from the Mesozoic Era, which is divided into three time periods. The first of these periods is the Triassic, which began about 250 million years ago and ended 208 million years ago. The second period is the Jurassic, which lasted from 208 million years ago to 145 million years ago. The last and longest period, the Cretaceous, started 145 million years ago and ended 66 million years ago. Each period is divided into three parts—early, middle, and late. *Stegosaurus* bones, for example, are found in rocks that were layers of sand and mud during the last part of the Jurassic period. So this makes *Stegosaurus* a late Jurassic dinosaur.

The oldest dinosaur bones are found in late Triassic rocks that are about 225 million years old. The Triassic was a time of great change for life on Earth. By studying the fossil remains of plants and animals found in Triassic rock, paleontologists are able to describe when and where different forms of plants and animals first appeared.

THE LAND OF PANGAEA

To understand what led to the appearance of the first dinosaurs, we must go back to the early Triassic. If we had a map of the Earth at that time, it would look very strange. It would show a giant ocean on one side and a giant continent on the other. All of our present continents, including North America, were part of that huge continent stretching nearly from the South Pole to the North Pole. North America lay at the northwest corner and was attached to Africa and South America. Geologists have named this supercontinent Pangaea, meaning "all Earth."

CYNOGNATHUS
TICINOSUCHUS

EARLY TRIASSIC ▪ Pangaea was centered on the warm equator. It was so large that cooling ocean breezes could not reach its interior. The sun's rays heated Pangaea's surface to very high temperatures. There were no large mountain ranges to block the flow of heated air, so all of Pangaea was warm. A great sandy desert filled the area where Utah, Arizona, and New Mexico are now.

Scientists who have studied Pangaea's weather systems believe that great tropical storms called monsoons formed over the ocean and swept inland. The rains ran quickly off the bare sand and rocks and into river valleys. The wet valleys and moist coastal areas were the only places where plants could grow.

Most of the plants in the early Triassic were survivors from forests that had once grown in huge swamps. The swamps were gone, but mosses, ferns, horsetails, and other earlier types of plants still lived in a few wet places. Two new kinds of plants were becoming more common — cycads and conifers. The cycads looked like very short palm trees, and the conifers looked like redwood trees. The leaves of these shrubs and trees had a tough outer layer that kept water inside the plant. They could survive in areas where rain fell only a few times a year.

Strangely enough, in the early Triassic, long before the dinosaurs, the most common reptiles looked like mammals. They had short snouts and compact bodies with short tails. And they had five toes on each foot like many mammals. They walked slowly with their long legs sprawling out to the sides. These mammal-like reptiles are called therapsids. Some scientists think that the bodies of the therapsids may have been covered with hair.

Another less common group of reptiles, the archosaurs, also lived in the early Triassic. Most archosaurs were small and walked with a clumsy waddle. They looked something like modern reptiles. Their thick leathery skin kept their bodies from drying out. Archosaurs could live in the dry conifer forests that were spreading through Pangaea. Throughout millions of years the archosaurs prospered, and many new forms of these reptiles appeared. Eventually, they lived up to their name, which means "ruling reptiles."

When an animal has features that allow it to survive in certain conditions, we say that it is adapted to those conditions. A polar bear, for example, is well adapted to life in the Artic. Its thick fur is an adaptation for cold air and icy water. Individual animals that are well adapted usually survive long enough to mate and produce young. Animals that are poorly adapted often die before they can produce another generation like themselves. As an environment changes, the animals in it must evolve slowly over many generations or they will become extinct.

MIDDLE TRIASSIC ▪ The archosaurs were well adapted to dry conditions; the mammal-like therapsids were not. Life became more difficult for therapsids in the middle Triassic, when Pangaea became even drier.

As the conifer forests spread, there was more food for plant-eating reptiles. As the plant eaters increased, so did carnivores, the animals that hunted them. Most of the meat-eating archosaurs in the middle Triassic looked like short-snouted, long-legged crocodiles. These 10-foot-long (3-meter) animals could run rather well. Their speed, large heads, and sharp teeth made them the most dangerous predators of their day.

ORNITHOSUCHUS

Some other archosaurs evolved differently. *Lagosuchus* is an example. It was a small and lightly built creature that ran on two legs. Strange as it seems, animals like these rabbit-sized reptiles evolved into gigantic dinosaurs!

LATE TRIASSIC ▪ Toward the end of the Triassic, Pangaea began to break apart. North America shifted westward away from Africa. The early Atlantic Ocean was a narrow seaway. In the southwest, a large forest covered the low-lying region that had been a desert in the early Triassic. Conifer trees grew to a great size, and many different kinds of animals lived there. Rivers and pools were filled with fish, large fish-eating amphibians, and reptiles.

The forest was often flooded by rivers that carried large amounts of mud. The floods buried plants and animals under thick layers of sediment. And from time to time, ash from volcanoes more than 100 miles (160 kilometers) away buried parts of the forest. The falling ash killed trees and shrubs and animals. But the forest grew back again and again.

The river mud and volcanic ash preserved a fossil record of late Triassic life in western North America. Part of this large region is now known as Arizona's Petrified Forest National Park. Petrified means "changed to stone." The Petrified Forest National Park is famous for its huge fossilized logs; it also contains North America's oldest dinosaurs.

The first dinosaurs were primitive two-legged meat eaters. They were 6 to 9 feet (2 to 2.5 meters) long. They had very thin long legs, like their archosaur relatives, and short compact bodies with large heads. These primitive dinosaurs from the Petrified Forest have not been named yet, but one skeleton found in 1984 has been given the nickname of Gertie! Fossil remains of primitive dinosaurs are very rare, but they have been found thousands of miles from one another. For this reason, paleontologists believe that the first dinosaurs spread rapidly across Pangaea.

Near the end of the late Triassic, other types of dinosaurs appeared in North America. The best known of these is *Rioarribasaurus* (formerly called *Coelophysis*). Its bones have been found in the Petrified Forest, but better specimens come from a spectacular dinosaur graveyard at Ghost Ranch in New Mexico. A single quarry there has produced more than one hundred skeletons.

Rioarribasaurus was a carnivore. Its long, slender jaws were lined with eighty teeth shaped like the blade of a knife. The back edge of each tooth had tiny sawlike points, like the serrations on a steak knife. Its hands, or front feet, had three sharp claws for grasping its prey.

Its lightly built skull had large open spaces between the upper skull bones—a feature found in nearly all carnivorous dinosaurs. Two openings provided enough space for the large eyes that predatory animals need to search for prey. Other openings were for powerful jaw muscles.

RIOARRIBASAURUS

Rioarribasaurus was 6 to 8 feet (2 to 2.5 meters) long with slender, hollow bones. It ran rapidly on its birdlike hind legs. The long, slender tail was held off the ground to balance the front part of the body at the hips. The backbone was firmly supported at the hips by five vertebrae (the small bones that make up the backbone). This was a stronger hip structure than the three or less vertebrae that earlier reptiles had.

The large number of *Rioarribasauruses* found together at Ghost Ranch probably means that they traveled in groups. Perhaps they hunted in packs like wolves. A few skeletons contained chewed-up bones of young *Rioarribasauruses*—cannibal dinosaurs!

In the last few million years of the Triassic, some important groups of animals appeared—crocodiles, pterosaurs (flying reptiles), and mammals. But paleontologists have discovered that many of the plants and animals that lived in the late Triassic had disappeared by the early Jurassic. This means that 208 million years ago, at the end of the Triassic, there was a great extinction, a time when many types of living things died out. The dinosaurs survived the late Triassic extinction, and in Jurassic times, some became the largest creatures to ever walk on land.

THE AGE OF DINOSAURS

Paleontologists have found and named hundreds of different kinds of dinosaurs. They have placed dinosaurs with similar features together in groups and have tried to learn the history of each group. This work is called classification. For example, all dinosaurs with four pillarlike legs, very long necks and tails, and small heads are placed in one group and called sauropods. The sauropods have a long history that begins with some medium-sized plant eaters in the late Triassic and continues with the giants of the late Jurassic and late Cretaceous. Other dinosaurs are not as well known and are more difficult to classify. This causes much discussion and disagreement among dinosaur experts.

All the experts agree, however, that all dinosaurs can be divided into two big groups depending upon the shape of their hip bones: saurischians and ornithischians. The saurischians had hips shaped like a lizard's, while the ornithischians had hips shaped like a bird's. The shape of the skulls and teeth are important in separating meat eaters from plant eaters. All of the bird-hipped dinosaurs ate plants, but the lizard-hipped dinosaurs can be divided into two groups—the meat-eating theropods and the plant-eating sauropods.

SAUROPODS ▪ Most of the sauropods were gigantic animals that walked on four legs. The largest of these, *Brachiosaurus* and *Diplodocus*, lived in the late Jurassic where the Rocky Mountains are today. Some scientists claim that the heaviest *Brachiosaurus* (nicknamed *Ultrasaurus*) weighed more than 100 tons. But other scientists don't believe that was possible. Their studies show that the leg bones would have broken under such a weight if the animal had moved faster than a slow walk. New estimates for the weights of the heaviest sauropods are about 50 tons.

BRACHIOSAURUS

DIPLODOCUS

TED FINGER

How much food did a 50-ton sauropod need to eat each day? The answer is an unbelievable 190 pounds (85 kilograms) of small twigs and leaves. Their sharp-edged teeth were good for clipping small branches, but they were not good for chewing. The leaves and twigs were swallowed whole. How was this coarse food digested?

No one knows for sure.

Paleontologists have to guess about the parts of dinosaurs that are not preserved as fossils — parts like the stomach, heart, and lungs. A lot of what scientists believe about the insides of dinosaurs they learned by studying the bodies of modern animals. For example, birds, which cannot chew food because they have no teeth, have special muscular sacks that food enters before passing on to the stomach. The walls of the sack (called a gizzard) are lined with small stones that the bird has swallowed. The gizzard crushes the food to a pulp before it is digested. Some sauropod skeletons have been found with many smoothly polished pebbles lying where the stomach would have been. Scientists think that the pebbles were swallowed to help crush the twigs and leaves that the sauropods ate.

The sauropods became extinct in North America in the early Cretaceous. But sauropods survived in South America. These southern sauropods moved north into western North America at the very end of the Cretaceous.

LARGE THEROPODS ▪ The first large theropod in North America was *Dilophosaurus*. It lived in the early Jurassic. It was about 20 feet (6 meters) long and weighed about 1,000 pounds (500 kilograms). It had a large head, and its mouth was filled with unusually long bladelike teeth. The head had two thin crests. The crests, which might have been brightly colored, were used as a display, perhaps to attract a mate.

DILOPHOSAURUS

At the end of the Jurassic, a much larger and fiercer theropod terrorized western North America. This was the 35-foot-long (11-meter) *Allosaurus*. Its huge mouth had serrated teeth for slicing flesh. Its jaws expanded sideways so it could swallow huge chunks of meat. Could this ferocious hunter kill the huge sauropods that lived at the same time? It seems more likely it would have preyed on smaller animals such as the slow-moving *Stegosaurus*.

The last great theropod, *Tyrannosaurus rex*, may have been the largest meat-eating animal that ever walked the Earth. (Scientists now believe that the newly discovered *Giganotosaurus carolinii*, which lived 30 million years before *Tyrannosaurus rex*, could have been about three tons heavier). *Tyrannosaurus rex* was about 45 feet (14 meters) long and weighed 6 to 7 tons. Its huge head was different from the heads of earlier meat eaters. The bones were thicker and stronger. The teeth were shaped like thick, pointed rods instead of like knife blades, and the eyes faced forward instead of looking to the side.

This was a head adapted for attacking and killing large animals. Its forward-looking eyes allowed it to judge the exact distance to the animal it was hunting. When the prey was close enough, the huge predator charged at it with its jaws wide open. The strong daggerlike teeth sank deeply into the flesh of its prey, and the powerful jaws crushed its bones. Such sudden violent attacks were necessary to bring down large plant eaters like *Triceratops*.

TYRANNOSAURUS REX

DEINONYCHUS

STENONYCHOSAURUS

SMALL THEROPODS ▪ In spite of their size, tyrannosaurs weren't the most dangerous predators. That honor belongs to a group of smaller, faster dinosaurs that are popularly called raptors. The best-known raptor is *Deinonychus*, whose name means "terrible claw."

This animal, whose fossilized remains have been found in Montana and Wyoming, walked on its hind legs and on only two of its three toes. The third toe had a very long, sharp, curved claw that was held off the ground. These huge claws were this predator's primary weapon. It had long grasping hands to hold its prey while the terrible slashing claws did their work. Its mouth was filled with sharp teeth. The jaw had two sets of muscles. One set was attached near the hinges of the jaw for a quick snapping bite. When the jaw was almost closed, a second set of muscles produced a powerful bite that could crush bones.

These incredibly fierce 10-foot-long (3-meter) predators might have hunted in packs, leaping onto the backs of large plant eaters or even carnivores.

DINOSAURS AND BIRDS ▪ Paleontologists have always noticed that the small theropods have many things in common with birds. Both could walk only on their hind legs. They both had long, slender, hollow leg bones, very flexible knee and ankle joints, large claws, and scales on their legs. Both had stiff backs and flexible necks. Both dinosaurs and birds laid eggs with hard shells. Birds, in fact, are the dinosaurs' closest living relatives.

When one creature looks like another, we say that it mimics it. One group of small theropods looks a lot like our modern flightless birds, the ostrich and emu. These theropods are called bird mimic reptiles, or ornithomimosaurs. They are slim, long-legged creatures, the fastest of all of the dinosaurs. *Struthiomimus*, whose name means "ostrich mimic," could probably have run at more than 30 miles (50 kilometers) per hour. It had a long flexible neck and a tiny head with a sharp toothless beak. It lived throughout Alberta, Canada, and probably ate fruits as well as insects, amphibians, lizards, and small mammals.

BIRD-HIPPED PLANT EATERS ▪ So far we have described the lizard-hipped dinosaurs, which include the giant sauropods and the meat-eating theropods. All of the rest of the dinosaurs were plant eaters, and they belong to the bird-hipped group. They include the four-footed stegosaurs and the armored and horned dinosaurs. They also include the two-footed plant eaters called ornithopods.

Iguanodon was an ornithopod that lived in South Dakota during the early Cretaceous. It was 33 feet (10 meters) long. It often walked on four feet, but when it was browsing on trees or defending itself from predators, it walked on two. The thumb on its hand had a large spike—an excellent defensive weapon.

Iguanodon had a toothless beak for clipping branches. The back of its mouth contained rows of teeth that could shred the toughest plants. Muscular cheeks kept the food in place for chewing.

Later ornithopods had a wide beak like the bill of a duck. Unlike ducks, the duck-billed dinosaurs had teeth. Many small teeth were packed tightly together to form large crushing surfaces. These banks of teeth turned plant food into pulp for easier digestion. Some duckbills had as many as 1,200 teeth!

IGUANODON

A duckbill nesting area from the late Cretaceous period was uncovered on a hill in Montana. The fossilized nests were shallow, scooped-out holes containing eggs carefully arranged in circular patterns with the ends pointing up. Bones and teeth of young duckbills were found on the same site. The teeth showed signs of wear from eating. It seems that the adult duckbills brought food to their young. This type of duckbill earned the name *Maiasaura*, which means "good mother reptile."

Stegosaurus must surely be the strangest bird-hipped dinosaur. It is easily recognized by the large diamond-shaped plates along its back and by its tail spikes. The spikes were certainly used as a weapon, but what was the purpose of the plates?

The plates were made of porous bone that grew in the animal's thick skin just like fingernails grow from skin on our fingers. They had channels that allowed blood to flow into the skin that covered them. Scientists believe that these plates helped *Stegosaurus* to regulate its temperature and prevent overheating in the hot Jurassic sun. Blood would cool quickly on the surface of the plates.

But on the other hand, if *Stegosaurus* needed to warm up, it could simply stand sideways to the sun. The sun's rays would then hit the flat surface of its plates and heat the blood in them. The blood would carry the warmth to the animal's muscles.

Ankylosaurus lived during the late Cretaceous in western North America. It was a low, wide animal completely covered with huge, thick, bony plates for protection.

The plates were not part of the animal's skeleton. They grew from the skin like the plates on *Stegosaurus*'s back. The end of its flexible tail had a heavy club of solid bone. This club could hit the leg of an attacking predator with enough force to break bones.

The largest *Ankylosauruses* were 33 feet (10 meters) long and weighed 6 tons.

ANKYLOSAURUS

TRICERATOPS

Triceratops was a giant plant eater weighing about 10 tons. At 30 feet (9 meters) long, it was the largest of the horned dinosaurs. The most impressive part of this animal was its head with its bony neck frill up to 8 feet (2.5 meters) long. Some of its neck bones were fused together to support the weight of its head. Tremendously powerful jaw muscles were attached to the frill. This was one plant eater with a very dangerous bite!

There was a short horn on *Triceratops*'s nose and a huge pair of horns above the eyes. These may have been used for fighting between males in contests of strength. The horns were also excellent protection against its great enemy *Tyrannosaurus rex*.

Triceratops lived during the final two million years of the Cretaceous, so it was among the last of the mighty dinosaurs.

THE END OF AN AGE

In the late Cretaceous, North America had a wonderful assortment of dinosaurs. The forests of Alberta and Montana were filled with the sounds of many different kinds of duckbills. Large herds of horned dinosaurs trampled the thick growths of tree ferns, bald cypresses, magnolias, and figs. It was a dinosaur paradise. Half of all the dinosaurs we know about lived in the late Cretaceous.

But by the end of the Cretaceous Period the world of the dinosaurs had begun to change. Sea levels were falling. The great inland sea that covered the center of North America during the late Cretaceous became smaller. All the continents that were once part of Pangaea were separating. Their movement opened deep sea passages that let cold ocean currents flow from the North and South Poles toward the equator.

STYRACOSAURUS

The climate began to cool during the last five to ten million years of the Cretaceous. The continuous summer of earlier times in North America was replaced by warm and cool seasons.

The subtropical jungles in the western states slowly changed to forests of hardier trees, such as walnuts and oaks. Herds of duckbills and horned dinosaurs traveled south in search of food as the days became shorter and cooler in the fall. The huge animals ate so much that they would destroy whole forests if they stayed in one place. By migrating with the changing seasons, they had more to eat all year.

Layers of rock near Hell Creek in Montana record the very last events of the Cretaceous Period. Paleontologists have found fossils from nineteen kinds of dinosaurs in the older bottom layers of these rocks. Younger layers farther up have fewer kinds of dinosaurs. In the uppermost Cretaceous rocks, only seven kinds of dinosaurs are found. The next layers of rock have no dinosaur fossils at all. This evidence shows that dinosaurs were slowly dying out for millions of years, and then suddenly the last ones became extinct. The wonderful animals that had ruled North America for 140 million years were gone.

A GREAT MYSTERY ▪ The extinction of the last dinosaurs is one of the great mysteries of nature. We don't know why it happened. We don't even know for sure how long it took. It may have taken only a few weeks or half a million years. We do know that whatever destroyed the dinosaurs also killed off many other living things. Ocean creatures, flying reptiles, and even some plants became extinct at the same time.

Some scientists think the extinction took a long time and was caused by a slow cooling of the climate. Many others think that the extinction was sudden and was caused by a huge meteorite from outer space striking the Earth.

They believe that the impact of the meteorite would have thrown millions of tons of dust into the Earth's atmosphere. The thick dust would have made day as dark as night. Without the sun's heat, temperatures all over the Earth would have dropped to below freezing. This darkness and cold could have lasted for weeks or even months, causing the extinction of plants and animals. When the dust finally settled, the sunlight and warmth would have returned, but life on Earth would never again be the same.

There are many scientists who disagree with the idea that a meteorite killed the dinosaurs. The discussion about the last dinosaur's extinction will go on and on until one day perhaps, the great mystery will be solved.

Nearly everyone is interested in the life and death of these great creatures. Their giant bones and fantastic skulls have always excited and challenged our imaginations. Looking at and learning about dinosaurs is fun, but it is also useful. By studying the ancient world of North America, we learn about the delicate balance between animals, plants, climate, and the Earth.

SCIENTISTS DIVIDE DINOSAURS INTO
TWO MAJOR GROUPS ACCORDING
TO THE SHAPE OF THEIR HIP BONES.
THE ORNITHISCHIANS HAD BIRDLIKE
HIPS, WHILE THE SAURISCHIANS
HAD LIZARDLIKE HIPS.

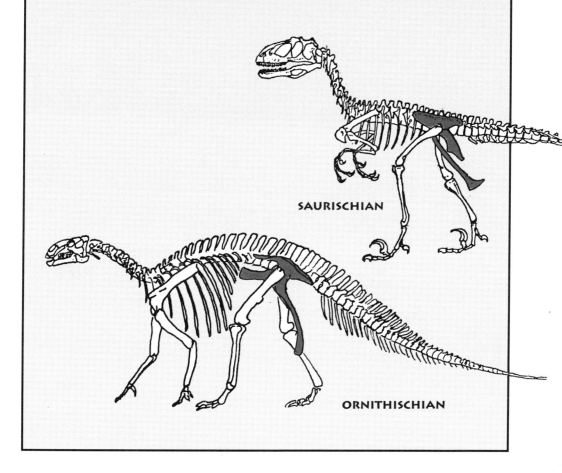

SAURISCHIAN

ORNITHISCHIAN

TIMELINE

Years Ago:

250 million	The Triassic Period begins. The Earth's climate is hot and dry.
225 million	The first dinosaurs appear.
215 million	*Rioarribasaurus* hunts in the Petrified Forest of Arizona.
208 million	The Jurassic Period begins. The Earth's climate gradually becomes wetter.
150 million	*Allosaurus, stegosaurus*, and the giant sauropods live in Wyoming and Colorado.
145 million	The Cretaceous Period begins.
120 million	The first flowering plants appear.
70 million	Many dinosaurs live in the warm, lush forests of Montana and Alberta, including *Triceratops* and *Tyrannosaurus rex*.
65 million	The dinosaurs become extinct.

Find Out More

Dinosaur Fossils by Alvin Granowsky (Austin, Texas: Raintree Steck-Vaughn, 1992).

Dinosaurs by Michael J. Benton (New York: Dorling Kindersley, 1993).

Dinosaurs by Mary L. Clark (Chicago, Ill.: Childrens Press, 1981).

Dinosaurs by Daniel Cohen (New York: Dell Publishing, 1993).

Dinosaurs by Claude Delafosse and James Prunier (New York: Scholastic, 1993).

Dinosaurs by Lee B. Hopkins (San Diego, Cal.: Harcourt Brace, 1990).

Dinosaurs by Christopher Maynard (New York: Kingfisher Books, 1993).

What Color Is That Dinosaur?: Questions, Answers, and Mysteries by Lowell Dingus (Brookfield, Conn.: The Millbrook Press, 1994).

Index